THE COZY CASE OF MURDER AND A TRUE FUREVER HOME

CURLY BAY ANIMAL RESCUE COZY MYSTERY
BOOK EIGHTEEN

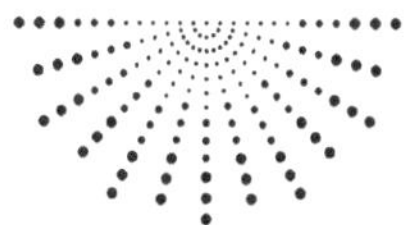

DONNA DOYLE

PUREREAD.COM

CONTENTS

CONTENTS

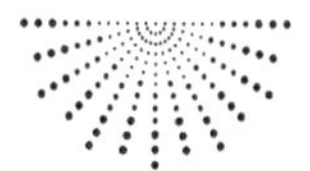

"Hold still, honey. You're almost there." Courtney ran her fingers down the head of a terrier mix who'd been brought into the Curly Bay Pet Hotel and Rescue by Officer Jacobs earlier that morning. She could still feel the layers of dirt caked into the dog's fur. Dora had decided to attack her massive knots with the clippers first, but the poor dog had been too terrified.

"I appreciate you holding her," the groomer commented as she carefully whizzed away another tight knot of dirt and fur. "Some of them will stand in the ties right off the street, but there was no way I was going to get her taken care of alone. As soon as I clipped her in, she started to throw a fit. She seems to like you, poor thing."

Courtney looked into the deep brown eyes of the creature. She was scared, for sure, but she'd calmed down a lot since Dora had called her into the grooming area. Courtney could see the hope burning dimly in those eyes, wondering if this time would be different. "Poor thing, indeed. Every time we get one in like this, I think it'll be the last time. But then there's always another one. I should be glad that my work never ends, but not this way. What do you think we should name her?"

After taking one final pass with the clippers, Dora turned them off. "Well, the weather is finally starting to get nice after that nasty winter. Maybe something spring-like?"

"That's a nice idea. How about Blossom?" Courtney kept her hands on the dog although Dora was done with the clippers, carefully moving her fingers back until she was scratching behind the canine's ears. The dog's eyes widened a little with fear, but once she realized what was happening, she closed her eyes and tilted her head to the side.

Dora laughed. "Blossom sounds good to me. Now let's see if she's as scared of a bath as she was the clippers.

Fortunately, Blossom had far less of a problem with

this part of the procedure. She watched every motion carefully, retreating to the corner of the tub here and there, but as long as they introduced her to each new thing slowly and carefully, she allowed them to wash all the dirt and grime down the drain.

"Blossom! You smell wonderful now!" Courtney kissed her on the nose. "I think everyone is going to love you! We'll have to make sure Oliver gets some great pictures of you, with a little flower tucked behind your ear and all!"

Just then, Jessi poked her head into the grooming area. "Courtney, phone's for you."

"I've got her from here," Dora assured her.

Giving Blossom one last scratch behind the ears, Courtney headed to her office. "Courtney Cain, how may I help you?"

"Hi, honey!"

"Mom? Is everything okay?" Courtney sat down quickly in her desk chair. Although they often spent time together chatting in the evenings, her mom rarely called while Courtney was at work. "Are you guys all right?"

"We're fine, sweetie. Just fine. Don't put that in that drawer, Randy. You'll never find it again."

Courtney smiled at hearing her mother's admonition toward her father. Her parents had always gotten along quite well, but these little exchanges were frequent. "So, what's going on?" she pressed, eager to know what warranted a call in the middle of the day. Something had to be happening.

"Well, we've decided to sell the house!"

Glad she was already sitting down, Courtney scrunched her brows together. "Really? You guys have been there forever."

"That's what I was thinking, too. But there's a hotel developer that's buying up this whole neighborhood. We have the option to sell now at a price that's above what the place is actually worth, or stick it out and see what happens to the value of the home after the hotel is built. Personally, I don't want some massive resort right in my backyard."

"Wow." Courtney could now understand why her mom had called. This was big news, indeed. "Is Dad okay with it?"

Cheryl Cain chuckled. "He's already talking about what we'll pack up first and which furniture we should keep! We were just wondering if you might be able to help us find a new place."

Courtney glanced down at her desk calendar. Her parents lived over an hour away in the city. She'd love to help them shop, and going around to look at homes with a realtor was a lot of fun. But when was she possibly going to have time? The shelter kept her constantly busy. "I'll be happy to do whatever I can, and I might be able to take off an evening here or there. Have you started looking online yet?"

"Ah, no. That's part of what we wanted your help with. It seems they pretty much put everything on the computer these days, and we're just not experienced with it."

Her shoulders relaxed a little. Poking around at home listings on the internet was something she could easily do when she was on her lunch breaks or curled up at home in the evenings with Peppa at her side. "Of course. I can send you the links for ones that you might be interested in."

"You're a darling!"

"That's my girl!" her father echoed in the background.

"It'll be fun." Courtney finished up the phone call and got off just as Lisa Patterson walked into the office.

"What's the matter?" her friend asked. "Are you not wanting to go out for lunch today after all?"

"Oh. Oh, is that time already?" Courtney glanced at the clock, shocked to see how quickly the morning had flown by. "Wow. Yes, I definitely still want to go to lunch." She grabbed her purse out of the bottom drawer of her desk. Peppa wagged her tail, and Courtney reminded her to be a good girl while she was gone.

"What's bothering you?" Lisa asked as they headed out toward her sedan.

There was no point in trying to hide it. Courtney had befriended Lisa shortly after she'd moved to Curly Bay. Being new to the place herself, the two of them had found quite a bit to talk about. They'd been best friends for a few years now. "My parents are selling their house. Well, they're being bought out by a developer, anyway. I don't blame them, but it's strange to think that all those childhood memories will be gone."

"No, they won't," Lisa insisted as she turned onto the main drag. "You'll still have all those memories. They'll probably just feel different when you no longer get to go back to the place where they were created."

"You're very philosophical about this," Courtney noted.

Lisa shrugged. "My parents sold their place several years ago, and I was a little weirded out by it, too. I've gotten past it, though. And hey, I've got some news that might at least get your mind off it for a little while."

"I'm listening."

"I just found out about this contest for community development projects. There's this non-profit organization, Change for Better, I believe it's called, and they're basically giving out this big sum of money to an organization that can show its impact on the community. I thought this would be the perfect chance for you to do some of the big changes you've talked about at the shelter."

Courtney drummed her knuckles against the window, instantly intrigued by the idea. She was constantly working on fundraising, and it was hard work. A big grant would make her life easier, and it would have a huge effect on the animals that she wanted so badly to help. "What do you have to do to enter?"

Her friend lifted a shoulder. "The instructions are pretty vague. You just have to send them some sort of presentation, video, slideshow, letter, or otherwise, to let them know why you deserve the money."

"Huh." Courtney was instantly working on ideas. She could feel excitement building in her stomach. "A video would be good. That way some of the animals could be included in it. And maybe I could get people from the community to give their testimonials. If we won, we might actually be able to put a new wing on the building and house more pets."

Pulling up in front of Salazar's Salad Bar, Lisa put the car in park. "You know you've already got me! We can come up with a list of other people we can talk to while we eat."

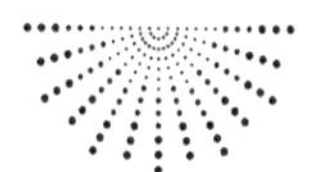

The next day, Courtney parked near city hall. She fetched Peppa from the backseat, knowing the dog would be more than welcome inside. After all, Peppa had saved Courtney's life here once, and everyone was used to seeing her around.

"You still have to be on your best behavior," Courtney reminded her as she straightened the blazer she'd put on that morning. "Mayor Powers knows us, but I still want to make a good impression."

They stepped inside, spoke to the secretary, and a few minutes later were ushered into Mayor Bridget Powers' office. It'd been redecorated since the last mayor was here. Everything was still very official, with the state and national flags on stands in the corner and a big oak desk, but floral prints on the wall and a new rug had given the place a slightly more feminine touch.

"Good morning, Courtney," Mayor Powers said as she set down her pen. She was dressed in a light pink suit that spoke of the beautiful spring weather. "I have to admit I was a little surprised when you said you wanted to come by. You usually just give me a ring on the phone. Hi, Peppa." She reached down a hand to pet the dog.

Courtney was reminded of the way she'd felt when she got that call from her mom in the middle of the day. "I didn't mean to worry you. I just thought this might be one of those things that's best done in person. I'd like your help with something."

Mayor Powers smiled and swept her short dark hair behind her ear. "Of course. You've helped me with plenty. I think I could return the favor."

"There's this contest." Courtney launched into a brief description of the Change for Better giveaway. "I feel like it would be more impactful if people from the community were in the video, instead of just me talking about the shelter. What better person than the mayor herself?"

Bridget nodded and folded her hands on the desk in front of her. "I think it's a wonderful idea, and you know you absolutely have my support on anything you want to do to continue on with your mission. There's no doubt in my mind that the shelter has made a huge difference in Curly Bay, both for the animals and the people."

Courtney had been spending a few years learning to read the body language of cats and dogs. They couldn't exactly speak to her and tell her what they were thinking. She was starting to notice, though, that this was a talent that carried over to humans quite easily. Courtney noticed the tension in Mayor Powers' shoulders and the hint of a frown at the corners of her mouth. "But?"

"But," Bridget said with a sigh, "I do have to tell you that you already have direct competition right here in town."

"Oh." Courtney sank back a little in her chair. "I figured there would be people all over the country vying for this money, so I guess I shouldn't be surprised that someone else here in Curly Bay has heard about it. Can I ask who it is?"

"I don't know if you've heard, but there's a man by the name of Julius Cline. He's purchased some land,

and he's planning to build a community center. It's over near the intersection of Pine and Logan. From what I can tell, it's that grant money you're talking about that would allow him to actually build the place. There are a lot of people around here who are really excited about it."

Courtney's heart flopped in her chest. She'd never been so disappointed to hear such good news. It would be easier to show the importance of a community center than it would an animal shelter, because it would affect so many people. She swallowed, though her throat was tight. "We don't have a lot of places around here to hold meetings or other events that don't charge a fee of some sort. I imagine the Scouts, youth groups, and other organizations are thrilled about it."

"They are," Mayor Powers agreed. "Now, don't think that's any reason for you to give up! I'm sure you'll still find plenty of people in Curly Bay who would be thrilled to help you. Just look at how many have adopted from you or fostered for you."

"That's true." Courtney shifted in her chair, feeling worried and uncomfortable. She laid her hand on Peppa's head to steady herself. "The problem is that every time I turn around, I'm just asking for money or help. I'm worried that people won't want to hear yet another plea for assistance."

Bridget pressed her lips together for a moment. Then she took a deep breath. "You know, I'm sure it does feel that way to you. I don't think it feels that way to everyone else, though. I think other people see you on social media or on the news and think, 'Hey, there's that lady who's always trying to get dogs and cats off the streets and into loving homes. That's great.' They might not always have the extra cash, or they might not have the extra room in their homes for a pet, but I do think they have a little more generosity when it comes to their judgement."

"That's very kind of you." Courtney was truly touched to know that someone like Mayor Powers felt that way, at the very least.

"I'm not being kind; I'm being honest," the mayor corrected with a smile. "Now then, I want you to pursue this project. I'm more than happy to help in any way I can, and you're free to use my name if you think it'll help coerce someone else into helping as well."

"Thank you." Twice in the same number of days now, Courtney felt like she'd had the rug pulled out from underneath her. Bridget's reassurances were helping, though. She stood up. "As soon as I get things figured out, I'll get back to you."

Bridget stood as well and gave another pet to Peppa. "You know, you may want to consider talking to Connie Gilbert."

"The writer?" Courtney had met her one summer while she was trying to track down a foster hound that wouldn't stop running away.

"That's the one," the mayor said with a nod. "She's been pretty busy helping to get the park museum started up, but she's an excellent writer. She might have a few ideas to help you out with your presentation."

"Thank you. I'll do that." Courtney left the mayor's office. The meeting hadn't exactly gone the way she'd expected, though she couldn't say it'd gone poorly. She still had Mayor Powers' backing, and now she had someone else she could contact to help her out. There was still quite a bit of work ahead of her, though, and only a short window of time to get it done. When she and Lisa had visited the Change for Better website, they'd discovered that all the presentations were due in less than two weeks.

"I guess we've got our work cut out for us," she said to Peppa as she buckled her into the passenger seat. "That means you'll probably get a lot of field trips."

The big beagle mix thumped her tail happily against the upholstery.

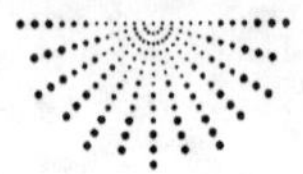

Courtney tapped her fingers on the steering wheel and chewed the inside of her cheek as she pulled out of her parking spot in front of City Hall. "I don't know who this Julius Cline is," she said to Peppa, "but it sounds like he might already have the money in the bag. Or at least, he has a better shot at it than I do. No offense, but I imagine they'll be more likely to support a community center than our place. I mean, not everyone is into animals. Not that I understand how anyone couldn't be." She reached over and stroked Peppa's short, soft fur. Courtney knew just how lucky she was that she got to take her dog almost everywhere with her. Most people didn't have that privilege.

Peppa bumped her head up under Courtney's wrist to encourage more petting.

"What's that? You think we might as well go drive by the site of the future community center and see what we're up against? Sounds like a plan to me. Hey, maybe we can hold adoption events there. That way, if we don't win the grant money, we still get some benefit from it." Courtney turned onto Pine Street.

She was on the outskirts of town in an area that was mostly residential. It wasn't where she would've imagined a community center to be built, but that wasn't exactly up to her. Courtney slowed down as she neared Logan Street, wondering if she'd be able to tell where the community center was going in. Skimming by several small houses, she noticed a smaller one set further back off the road. One side of the roof was sinking in, and weeds from last summer still gathered in clumps near the foundation. The gravel of the driveway was sinking slowly down into the dirt, but a luxury sedan sat on it. Courtney saw the name Cline one the license plate and immediately swung in. If this wasn't the right place, then maybe whoever was here could direct her.

"Stay here, baby," she said softly to Peppa. "I'll be right back."

Peppa was sitting upright in the passenger seat, obviously noticing that they were in a new place and wondering what was happening. She jutted her head forward and gave a soft woof.

Courtney turned in the direction the dog was looking to see an older man striding back and forth on the front porch, holding a cell phone to his ear. "It's all right, Peppa. I won't be but a minute."

Making sure she had her keys in her pocket, Courtney got out of the car. The man who she presumed to be Julius Cline gave no indication that he'd seen her, and instead his dress shoes thumped on the old wooden boards. He tugged at his already loosened tie with one hand. "I don't owe you anything further than what I've already done! Do you hear me? We had a deal, and I fulfilled my end of it. If you don't like it, then maybe you should've thought about that a long time ago!" He whipped the phone away from his face, squinted at the keys, and carefully used one finger to end the phone call.

"It doesn't quite have the same impact as slamming the receiver down, does it?" Courtney asked.

He jumped a little as he turned, but he smiled as she tucked his phone away in his pocket. "No, I can't say that it does. Can I help you with something?"

"Maybe." Courtney glanced around, wondering how a dilapidated site like this could've been chosen as the future location of a community center. It did sit on a rather large lot, being at the edge of town. In fact, it was far bigger than probably any of the other lots around it. She wondered if the field behind it would end up being purchased as an add-on later. "Are you Julius Cline?"

Coming down the porch steps, the man put his hand on the railing. He pulled it back quickly as he realized the railing was less stable than he was on his own. "I am."

"It's nice to meet you. I'm Courtney Cain." She held out her hand and he shook it. His grip was firm, but his hands were very soft. "I'd heard this is where the community center is being built, and I was curious about it."

Julius retrieved a handkerchief from his other pocket and dabbed his forehead with it. "That's the plan, anyway. It'll probably be some time before it goes up, though. You know how these things get, all caught up in red tape and supply costs."

Courtney debated on whether or not she should tell him that she planned to enter the same contest he was. After all, she didn't want him to think she was trying to intimidate him or coerce him into withdrawing his entry. "I run an animal shelter here in town, and I was wondering if the community center might be a place where we can hold adoption events."

"Oh. My goodness, the sun is warming up quickly today, isn't it?" Mr. Cline dabbed at some more perspiration on his temple. "That very well may be the case, young lady."

The more she thought about it, the more excited Courtney got despite the fact that this community center could take away her chances at winning the money. It would be a big benefit to Curly Bay, and mostly likely to the shelter as well. "Can I ask what the plans are?"

"Hmm?" Mr. Cline had taken his cell phone out of his pocket and glanced at the screen. He tucked it away again.

"The plans for the community center," she pressed. "Is it going to be a very big building? Something small? It looks like you'd have a decent amount of room here for parking, which is always difficult around here." Courtney surveyed the land, wondering just how people decided how to take a plain piece of land and turn it into something more.

"Modest, you could say. The, um, the plans are still in the works. Being drawn up and all that."

"Well, it's wonderful of you to want to do something like this for Curly Bay. I don't think many people would have that much generosity. I assume you plan to tear down this old house here?" Courtney reached out and touched one of the heavy posts that held up the roof over the front porch. It was one thing on the home that remained solid, but there were so many other elements that hadn't.

This part, at least, was something Julius was certain of. He bobbed his head as he turned to observe the old place as well. "Oh, absolutely. That'll have to come down right away."

Tapping her finger against her lip, Courtney's mind was working as she tried to imagine the house deleted from the scene, the grass trimmed, and some of it paved over with asphalt or concrete. "I know this is presumptuous of me, but if you'd like any input on ideas for the layout of the community center, I'd be happy to help. After running the shelter for a few years and doing various adoption events, I've noticed what's lacking in some buildings we've rented out, as well as what's been very helpful in others. I'm no expert, but I do have some experience on this end of things."

"Perhaps." Mr. Cline began dabbing at his forehead once again. "It's all still very early on, you know."

"I know," Courtney admitted. "I'm just very excited, and I know the rest of the town is, as well. It's not often that we get an opportunity like this. I'm sure you'll have a whole line of people waiting to request some space here, and I fully plan to be one of them." Perhaps Mayor Powers had been right when she said people weren't tired of her constantly asking for help and funds, but it wouldn't hurt to change up the venue a bit.

"That's very nice, young lady, but it's all still quite a ways off."

"Maybe so, but I know how fast Cooper's Construction can throw up a building when they're motivated," Courtney noted.

"Listen, I plan to hire a manager to run things, and I wouldn't want to speak for him. The only thing I'm doing is providing the land, and it's caused rather a stir. But I ask that you just be patient, and when the day comes, I'm sure you can reserve your spot. Now, if you'll excuse me, I really must be going." He gestured toward their vehicles.

Courtney felt all the excitement she'd managed to build up about the community center suddenly deflate. "Of course. Thank you for your time." She quickly hopped back in her car, where Peppa gave her a cursory sniff-down, and backed out onto the street.

"I think he was trying to avoid telling me that he's not willing to host shelter events there," she speculated to the dog as they headed back to the Curly Bay Pet Hotel and Rescue. "Did you see him? He started sweating bullets as soon as I told him who I was. I'd bet he already knew I was planning to enter the Change for Better contest. Either that, or he simply assumed it because we're another non-profit. Even so, it doesn't seem very fair to exclude us from using the place once it's built, because you know he's going to win."

At the next stop sign, she turned to see Peppa giving her a doleful look.

"You're right." Courtney smiled and put her arm around her dog. "I'm getting down on myself, and I don't know for sure what's happening just yet. I'll try to work on that. I promise."

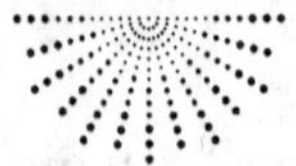

CHAPTER FOUR

Fortunately, although Courtney felt like her meeting with Julius Cline had been a dead-end, her primary mission of winning the community project money was still alive and kicking. Connie Gilbert had eagerly agreed to meet her as soon as the next day for lunch.

"Thank you so much for taking time out of your day and joining me," Courtney said as they took their seats at Russo's Pizza.

"Arc you kidding me?" Connie flipped her long dark hair behind her shoulders as she settled down into the booth. "I'd be crazy to pass up a chance at these garlic bread sticks. I tend to spend too much time holed up at my desk with a mug of coffee while I'm writing, and it's nice to get out and chat."

"I'd think you'd be out and about quite a bit while you're working on starting up the museum," Courtney noted.

The waiter came by to take their drink orders, and when he was gone, Connie shook her head. "I am, but it's not as much of a field trip as you might think. I want to have everything as well researched as possible. Say, for instance, if we're going to have a display about the life of Beryl Mullins, I want it all to be accurate. Plus, there are a lot of phone calls to make and emails to send. I do enjoy it, though," she made sure to add.

"I'm sure you do, and I know a lot of people are excited about it."

Connie phone beeped, and she smiled and pointed at it when she checked the screen. "Randy Shephard is probably the most excited about it," she said, naming off the park manager. "He and I have been working together pretty closely on this project, and I swear he's got a new idea for it every day."

Courtney raised an eyebrow, wondering if there might be something more between the pretty writer and the athletic park director than creating a museum, but she didn't know either of them well enough to say anything. "With as much work as the museum is, I almost hate to talk to you about the main reason I contacted you."

The waiter returned with their drinks and disappeared again when he had their orders, which he promised would be out to them as quickly as possible.

"Go right ahead," Connie insisted. "I like to be busy."

"There's this organization called Change for Better," Courtney began, realizing as she tried to explain the contest that she was going to need to find a streamlined, easy way to lay it all out for everyone she talked to. So far, she'd only had to describe it to Mayor Powers and Connie, but if things went right, she'd be talking to many more people than that.

"At any rate," she went on, "Mayor Powers suggested you might have some ideas for the presentation. She thinks highly of you and your talents. I don't want you to feel obligated in any way, but if there's something you can help with, I'd greatly appreciate it."

"Interesting," Connie mused. She sat back as the waiter returned with their orders, and she picked up her fork and began swirling her shrimp scampi around it. Steam rose up in front of her. "You know, I used to do a little grant writing when I was younger. It wasn't always my favorite work, but the reward was definitely there. I'm not sure exactly *what* I can do, but I'm sure I can come up with something."

"It really would mean the world to me. I know there's probably a ton of competition out there, plus I've found out that I've got competition just down the street for the new community center." Courtney frowned at her tortellini, once again thinking about her impromptu meeting with Julius Cline. She'd promised Peppa she'd put it behind her and not worry about it, but that was proving a much harder thing in practice.

"I did hear about that," Connie admitted with a nod as she picked up her napkin and dabbed at the corner of her mouth. "About the community center, anyway, but not the contest."

"I must really be behind," Courtney noted. "I'd only just heard about it yesterday."

"I actually tried to get Julius Cline to talk to me about the project. I thought it would make a great article for my blog. It's the sort of feel-good piece that people like to read without it being too fluffy, and of course my work lately revolves around local life."

"Tried?" That was the one word that caught Courtney's attention. It seemed to her that anyone who was being offered free publicity—whether for work or for non-profit project—would be willing to take it. "He wouldn't do it?"

Connie shrugged and plucked a breadstick from the basket on the table. "He said he had to fly out to New York for a business meeting and wasn't available. I thought that was kind of rude considering he's trying to get support for this big community project. I mean, sure, we all have schedules, but he could've found a little time for me. That's his loss, though."

"He didn't seem all that keen on talking to me, either," Courtney noted. "I have a feeling he thought I was scoping out my competition. I was in a way, but I was also genuinely just trying to let him know I supported the idea and that I'd want to do events there. The more I talked to him, though, the more agitated he got."

"Maybe he just doesn't like animals," Connie said with a grin. "I do, though. Let's talk a bit more about your contest entry. How does this work?"

Courtney bit her lip. "The entrance rules are kind of loose, so I could do whatever I want. I thought a video would have a big impact, and that maybe I could get people around town to talk about their experience with the shelter and what it's meant to them. It'd be good if it wasn't just a random series of clips, though, if it was almost more of a documentary than that."

Connie was bobbing her head already. "More cohesive than that," she agreed, tapping her fingertips together. "Perhaps a narrator, unraveling the story of the shelter in between testimonials."

"Yes!" Courtney slapped her hand over her mouth and giggled when she realized how loud she'd spoken. Fortunately, the other patrons in the restaurant didn't seem to be paying any attention to her. "I'm sorry. I'm just excited!"

"As you should be!" Connie set her fork down. She retrieved a small notepad and a fountain pen from her purse. "I think letting people talk about their own stories is the best way to go, but we can make it a more polished piece. Tell me everything you can think of when it comes to the shelter."

"Everything?" Courtney raised an eyebrow, but she could feel her hope for this contest rising up in her chest once again. "That could take a while."

Connie waved at her to go ahead. "Indulge me. It'll keep me from getting cramped up while I sit at my desk all afternoon."

"Let's see. I guess I'll start at the beginning." Courtney easily lost herself in the story of the Curly Bay Pet Hotel and Rescue, the job that'd started out simply as a replacement for the one she'd lost but that she'd soon realized had rescued her from the drudgery of corporate life. She talked of the dogs and cats—and even a few reptiles—that she'd had a hand in rescuing over the years, and the warmth she felt in her heart every time she saw the way her work changed the lives of both the pets and the people who took them in. Connie was a good listener, writing quickly with her fountain pen and nodding her encouragement, and the next thing Courtney knew, she'd spent far too long at lunch.

By the time she finally managed to make herself get up from the table and head back to work, though, Courtney felt thoroughly blessed. Her position at the shelter was so much more than a paycheck, and it'd been wonderful to have the chance to really tell someone about it.

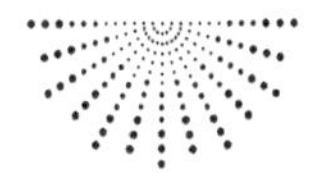

"She's going to help?" Jessi asked enthusiastically when Courtney returned from her lengthy meeting with Connie.

"That seems to be the case. If not, then she took a lot of notes for nothing." Courtney was feeling so much better about the Change for Better contest than she had just a day before after she'd discussed the upcoming community center with Julius Cline. There was always a chance that they wouldn't win, but having a professional like Connie on their side couldn't hurt. "I know it's a very dim hope, but I'd absolutely love to win."

"Win? Win what?" Mrs. Throgmorton asked as she strutted in through the front doors. The wealthy woman was dressed in a designer jogging suit in pale blue. Sir Glitter, the prize-winning Pomeranian tucked under her arm, was wearing a matching set. "We're all winners, if you ask me."

"Not in this case," Courtney amended. She grabbed the computer mouse and checked Sir Glitter in for his appointment. He was one of their regulars, as Mrs. Throgmorton always wanted him to receive the utmost care and pampering. "I'm entering the shelter in a contest for some grant money that could really make a difference around here."

"Oh? That's very exciting, dear!" She pushed her sunglasses back so that they rested in her silver hair. "This is a wonderful place. I'm sure you'll be a shoo-in!"

"Not when you consider that it's a national competition," Courtney replied. "I don't want to be a downer about it, but I do want to be realistic. The chances of us winning are very slim. However, you might be just the person to help us increase our odds."

"I'm listening!" Mrs. Throgmorton kissed her dog's nose and handed him to Dora when she came out of the grooming room to fetch him. "You know I'm always up for helping you out in any way I can."

Once more, Courtney explained her idea of putting

together a video, thinking she really ought to type out a flyer or have Nathan make her a website or something. "I'd like to get as many people on board with it as I can."

"I'm sure they'd all be delighted to participate, but I certainly don't mind using the fullest extent of my influence and affluence to get them to cooperate," Mrs. Throgmorton said with a smile. "That might sound a little harsh, I know, but I've been spending quite a bit of my adult life leveraging my wealthy acquaintances into prying open their wallets and giving to charity."

"And does that mean this will be harder or easier, considering you're asking them to go on camera instead of writing a check?" Courtney had no doubt that Mrs. Throgmorton really would do everything within her ability to make this presentation the best it could possibly be. This wasn't quite the same as a silent auction or a fundraiser dinner, though.

"Don't underestimate the power of a few minutes of fame, even if no famous directors will actually see it," Mrs. Throgmorton said with a wink. "Besides, if you do win, people would probably be thrilled to say they've been a part of it. Especially if it means they're not forking any money over."

"Sounds like you've got it all figured out," Jessi noted admirably.

"Indeed, we do," Mrs. Throgmorton confirmed.

"Maybe not all of it." Courtney didn't want to be the bearer of bad news, nor did she want anyone to think she was feeling too insecure, but there was still the other matter of this contest that had be discussed. She felt particularly obligated to disclose all the details to Mrs. Throgmorton, since she was so willing to help. "I understand that Julius Cline has also entered the contest."

"Julius Cline?" The older woman furrowed her brows together and leaned forward a bit. "What on earth did he enter for?"

"The new community center," Courtney explained. "I just heard of it the other day, but I figured you'd already know."

"I didn't, but then again, I have been rather busy planning my vacations this year. My travel agent didn't tell me, so I had no idea." She adjusted the heavy diamond ring on her finger.

Courtney sighed. "I actually went to talk to him the other day. I went by the future construction site, figuring at the very least I'd be able to have some adoption events at the community center, but Mr. Cline wasn't very keen on talking to me."

Now Mrs. Throgmorton's brows drew closer together. "Why ever not?"

"I don't know, but the more I talked about it, the less he seemed interested in listening. Then he said he had to be rushing off, so I left."

The wealthy woman smacked the edge of the counter in frustration, making her bracelets jangle. "That's just the silliest thing I've ever heard! A community center is just that! It's for the *community!* If he's going to be all high-handed about it, then he shouldn't be building it at all. Come on, dear. We're going to go talk to him."

"What, right now?" Courtney hadn't been surprised that Mrs. Throgmorton agreed to help with their contest entry, but this was definitely not what she'd expected.

"Of course! You said yourself there's only so much time before you have to turn your video in, and we might as well figure out what's really going on with him before we get elbows-deep into contacting people for endorsements." She hefted her purse a little further up onto her shoulder. "You can come with me, so we can all talk about this together."

Fully aware that she'd already been gone from the office too long, Courtney shook her head. "I really shouldn't—"

"I'm sure Jessi has the place handled?" Mrs. Throgmorton looked pointedly at the shelter worker.

A small smile tugged at the corners of Jessi's mouth at seeing her boss's obvious distress. "It should be just fine. We'll take care of Peppa and Sir Glitter while you ladies are gone."

"All right." Courtney relented and followed Mrs. Throgmorton out to her Cadillac. Her stomach did a flop as soon as she remembered the last time she'd written with the pet hotel's most loyal customer, but there was no backing out now. "I mean, if you're sure you have time."

"Time to help such a wonderful place get the funding it so sorely needs? Of course! I can call my travel agent back any time." She gave a hard flick of her wrist to turn over the engine, slapped the gear shifter into reverse, and shoved the pedal down. With a quick turn of the steering wheel that left Courtney's eyeballs rotating in her skull, she careened toward the main road. "Now then, where did you say the community center is being built?"

"Near the corner of Pine and Logan." Courtney clenched the leather upholstery of her seat with her hand, not wanting her friend to know how nervous she was about her driving. When Mrs. Throgmorton whizzed out onto the road right in front of oncoming traffic, however, she wrapped her fingers tightly around the grab handle above the window. "I don't see why he would be there, though. I think I was just lucky enough to find him the other day."

"It's worth a look, and if he's not there, then we'll try his house. I can't say that I know him supremely well, but I do know him, and I'm not shy at all about talking some sense into him." Slamming on the brakes, Mrs. Throgmorton flung the car onto a side street.

Courtney gulped, just hoping they would make it there alive. "I thought maybe he heard I was entering the same contest, and that was why he didn't want to offer any help to the shelter. Competition and all that."

"Nonsense!" There was another massive engagement of the brakes as a squirrel ran out in the middle of the road. It took one look at the giant grille heading toward it and skittered back the way it'd come. "There should be no such thing as competition when you're talking about things like this! He can get over it, and then he can commit to allowing you to have events there."

"You really don't have to do this. It might only make him more angry with me, and then he'll be angry with you, too." Courtney wondered why she hadn't insisted on driving.

"Darling, by the time I'm done with him, he'll probably be begging to be featured in your video," the older woman replied confidently. "Somewhere near here, is it?"

"Right down here. You see that run-down house? That's the place." She pointed down the street to the familiar structure, which stood out like a sore thumb amongst the nice bungalows that surrounded it.

"I see." With a hard swing to the left, Mrs. Throgmorton lurched the Cadillac into the driveway.

"He must not be here," Courtney said, noting there was no vehicle in sight beyond the one they were in.

"Let's have a look around anyway. I'm curious about the place. It seems like an odd spot for a community center." She frowned as she threw the car into park and got out.

Courtney joined her. A bit of a breeze had kicked up, but she was grateful. It really had been a bit warm when she'd encountered Julius Cline here, and she needed a bit of a cooldown after that harrowing ride. "He told me they'd be tearing this old house down."

"I don't like it," Mrs. Throgmorton announced almost instantly.

"You don't like what?"

"The location!" The older woman flung her arms out at her sides in frustration. "A community center needs to be somewhere that the whole town can access it easily. Out here in the middle of a residential neighborhood is just absurd placement!"

Courtney shrugged. "I'm guessing he probably got the land cheap, considering the state of it." She skirted around an overgrown bush that tried to slap her in the face with its long, slender limbs.

"Even so, he's not doing Curly Bay as much of a favor as he wants to let on," Mrs. Throgmorton asserted. Perhaps a set of apartments would do nicely here, or just a new home. I don't know what he's thinking." She clucked her tongue and shook her head.

Courtney's eye was on the detail of the home itself. She'd always been somewhat intrigued by old structures, although she didn't know the first thing about them. Mrs. Throgmorton followed her as she skirted around the side of the house, heading down the driveway toward the lopsided detached garage that practically sat in the backyard. "I wonder what the story is here?"

"Oh, it's probably no real story at all," Mrs. Throgmorton said with a casual wave of her hand. "Someone couldn't pay their taxes, or they passed on or didn't want the home anymore. I know empty houses have a certain amount of romanticism about them, but—What's *that?*"

Courtney turned around to see what Mrs. Throgmorton was staring at. She fully expected to find a frog or a bug, or maybe some old car part that'd never been picked up when the last residents left the place. Instead, she saw a pale thing sticking out from the overgrown grass. It took her a long moment of staring at it before she'd allow her brain to register the fact that it was a hand. "Oh, no."

Mrs. Throgmorton tentatively stepped further toward it, peering through the grass. "Why, it's Hugh McGowan!"

CHAPTER SIX

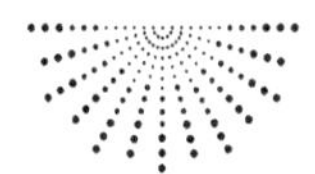

"Who's Hugh McGowan?" Courtney sat in the passenger seat of Mrs. Throgmorton's Cadillac. Her stomach was churning, but this time it didn't have anything to do with her friend's driving skills. Sirens wailed in the distance, drawing steadily closer.

"You don't know?" Mrs. Throgmorton leaned against the headrest. "He's one of the most prominent hotel magnates in the whole country."

Courtney swallowed, but it didn't make the horrid feeling in the back of her throat go away. "You know him?"

"I've stayed at plenty of the luxury resorts he's built, but I can't say I know him personally. I'm Curly Bay wealthy, after all, not New York wealthy. Oh, look.

Here they all come now. Curly Bay's finest." She rubbed her temple as the sirens screeched into the driveway and finally shut off.

Detective Fletcher was the first one to greet them at the vehicle as they got out. "Hello, ladies," he said in that somber tone of his. "I can't say this is a pleasant way to catch up with you. Can you tell me what happened?"

"We were just coming out here to talk to Julius Cline," Mrs. Throgmorton began to explain. She leaned against the door of her car and steepled her fingers over the bridge of her nose. "I suppose you already know he bought this property, and this was where Courtney found him the other day."

"Is he here?"

"We haven't seen him." Courtney noticed Fletcher give a quick nod to another officer, who headed back to his squad car and began making phone calls.

"At any rate, we just thought we'd have a look around, and, well, you know the rest." Mrs. Throgmorton pointed off in the direction where they'd found the body. "It's just unbelievable. Hugh McGowan!"

This put a stunned look on Detective Fletcher's face, and Courtney knew him to be a man who hardly changed his expressions at all. "The hotel guy?"

"That's the one! Can you believe it? I hardly do, except that I know what I saw. I'd go look again to make sure, except that I think I've seen enough!" She pressed her manicured hand to her mouth.

"Huh." Fletcher squinted at the paramedics, who were busy doing their job over where Courtney and Mrs. Throgmorton had found the body. "I can't imagine what a man like that would've been doing here."

"Me, neither!" the older woman exclaimed. "We're talking about a man who has seen all the most famous places in the world. London, Paris, and more! Not just seen them, but singlehandedly helped to develop them and cultivate their tourism with his amazing resorts! Why, he's the sort of man that I wouldn't think would even dream of setting foot in a small town like Curly Bay. Personally, I'd be embarrassed to meet him here. I love this town, Detective, but who would want to come here?"

"Indeed. And what, exactly, were you two ladies here for?"

Courtney thought perhaps she ought to take over

their report, since Mrs. Throgmorton was beginning to get visibly rattled. "I had spoken with Mr. Cline the other day about his plan to build a community center here, and we wanted to ask him a few more questions. You see, we're both entering this community development contest, and—"

Another car swung into the driveway, one that she recognized as belonging to Julius Cline. The newcomer had Detective Fletcher's attention as he hurried out from behind the wheel and rushed over. "Please don't tell me that what the young man said on the phone is true," he said as he surveyed the scene. "That someone died here?"

"I'm afraid so, Julius," Mrs. Throgmorton responded. She took his hand in both of hers. "I'm so sorry!"

Detective Fletcher cleared his throat. "I take it that means you really do own this property?"

"I do," Julius replied dully.

"And this was where you were going to build a community center?" Fletcher asked.

"That was the plan." He flapped his arms in the air uselessly. "It was so nice to retire, and I just wanted to give back to the community, but now some stranger has been killed here! This is horrible!"

Mrs. Throgmorton put a friendly arm around the landowner. "To make matters even worse, dear, I'm afraid that the victim is—"

The detective cleared his throat again. "Ma'am, perhaps you could give me a moment to speak with Mr. Cline alone?"

Realizing the faux pas she was about to make, Mrs. Throgmorton released Julius from her grip and stepped away. "Of course."

Courtney waited with her near the Cadillac while the two men moved off to talk in private. "This has certainly turned in a strange day."

"You're telling me!" Mrs. Throgmorton agreed. "I can't bear to think how poor Julius is going to react once he hears that this wasn't just some random stranger but a *famous* stranger! That's going to be horrible for him."

"I'm sure." Courtney filled her cheeks and blew out a long breath, looking for anything they could talk about besides Hugh McGowan's corpse. It wasn't the first time she'd seen one, but she found that experience didn't make things any easier. "Mr. Cline mentioned he was retired. What did he do for a living?"

Mrs. Throgmorton shook out her arms and rolled her shoulders. "I believe he was involved in some sort of investments, something that required a lot of travel. I can't say I know much of anything about it, other than the fact that he was gone a lot."

"I'm sure that was interesting," Courtney murmured for lack of anything better to say.

Looking over her shoulder toward the scene of the crime and then quickly looking away again, Mrs. Throgmorton focused on her nails and rings. "I have to wonder if this will put a stop to the community center altogether. That could be nice for you, if it means you end up winning the contest."

Courtney didn't like what that implied. "I'm not sure that's a price I would've wanted to pay," Courtney noted. "And I'd much rather have the community center built, even if I wasn't allowed to host any events there."

"Of course, dear. Of course. My mind is just wandering off in all directions, looking for something to do. This is rather unsettling."

"I know." Courtney squeezed her arm in sympathy. The paramedics were getting ready to leave, and when she glanced over at Detective Fletcher, she could see that he was finishing up with Julius Cline.

Mrs. Throgmorton saw that, too, because she took a step toward the two men as they broke apart. "I just want to give Julius my sympathy once more."

Fletcher stepped over to Courtney. "Well, well. You've stumbled upon quite the case this time. A deliriously wealthy hotel magnate murdered on the shabby lawn of an old home that's supposed to be nothing more presumptuous than a community center. What do you make of it?"

"I don't know," Courtney replied honestly. "I've been so busy with this contest, and now it's gotten me here."

"Oh, right. Tell me a little bit more about that." As the other emergency vehicles left, the detective listened carefully to everything Courtney had to say about the Change for Better competition. He tucked his hands in his pockets and nodded when she was done. "I don't have any good ideas for how to help, not like your friend Ms. Gilbert, but I'm certainly willing. Call me if you need me."

"I will." Courtney climbed back in the passenger seat, feeling only a little relieved that this part of the event was over. It was always intimidating when all the lights and sirens came down the road, especially when she knew they were coming toward her.

Somehow, though, things only felt more lonely now that they'd gone. She was left wondering what to do with what little information she had, and if it would do her any good at all.

"Let's get back." Mrs. Throgmorton was subdued as she turned the ignition. She slowly backed out of the driveway and cruised slowly across town.

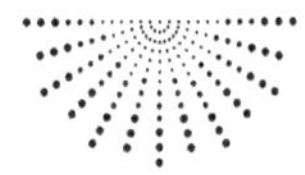

"Hi, honey!"

"Hi, Mom." Courtney's heart dropped when she took the phone call. She'd promised she'd help them find a home, and she'd hardly had any time to look at all. "Listen, I'm sorry I haven't been in touch with you. I think I might be able to find some time this evening to get online and look. I started to the other night, but I fell asleep." She'd awakened an hour or so later, glad to find that she'd dropped her phone next to her on the pillow instead of on her face.

"That's quite all right. Can you hear me okay from the car?"

Courtney held the phone away from her ear and turned the volume down a notch. "Yeah, Mom. I can hear you just fine. Where are you guys headed? Did you find a place?" Relief moved through her. She might've dropped the ball a little, and she knew that if her parents had any idea what else was going on in her life, they'd instantly forgive her, but it was still nice to know they were making progress.

"Tell her, honey!" her father encouraged from the driver's seat. "You don't want to wait until we're on her doorstep!"

Her doorstep?

"We're on our way to Curly Bay right now," her mother announced.

Courtney blinked. She loved her parents, and she'd happily welcome them into her home anytime they wanted to come by. It wasn't really like them to do so without calling first, more like a week in advance instead of when they were already on the road. "Why are you coming here?"

She could hear the smile in her mother's voice when she replied. "Well, we decided we might not want to stay in the city after all. We'll tell you all about it when we get there. We'll only have a little bit of time to chat, though. We're supposed to meet up with a real estate agent. I actually found her online! Me! Aren't you proud?"

"Yeah, Mom. That's great." It really was, considering how her parents had struggled with the swiftly advancing technology that was constantly shaking things up. And she wasn't upset that they wanted to check out some houses near her. It was all just so new. "I'm guessing it's Carolyn Davis?"

"How did you know?"

Courtney pressed her hand to her forehead and laughed a little. "It's a small town. There aren't exactly a lot of realtors, and there aren't exactly a lot of homes for them to sell. Tell me where you're meeting her, and I'll be there."

"Nonsense!" her father called out. "We'll pick you up!"

Half an hour later, they rolled into the driveway. Courtney came outside to meet them at their car. "I have to say, this is quite a surprise."

"The whole thing about selling the house was quite a surprise, too," her mother replied, "but here we are!"

Her father grabbed her in a bear hug. "How's my cupcake, other than surprised?"

"I'm good, Dad. Let's get inside and we can talk about this." Fortunately, Courtney had the day off work. She'd needed it desperately, both to catch up on some sleep and to hopefully start doing more work on her contest entry. Apparently, she also needed it to go house hunting, as well.

"No time for that!" Cheryl Cain held open the back door of the car. "We've got to go meet Carolyn, but we can talk in the car. Hop on in!"

Clipping Peppa onto a leash and grabbing her purse, Courtney was quickly on her way for an impromptu home visit. "Okay, you've kept me in suspense long enough," she said as she buckled in. "You guys have *got* to tell me why you're thinking about moving to Curly Bay!"

"Well, you keep talking about what a great little town it is, for one thing," her father offered. "You're always going on about how people support each other, and all locally owned businesses. It just makes us wonder what we might be missing if we stay in the city. I can't say I'm interested in fighting traffic every time I need to run to the pharmacy, either."

"Plus, we miss you," her mother admitted.

Courtney reached up and patted her arm. "I miss you guys, too. I just don't want you to do something too rash that you might regret. You've been in the city forever."

Randy Cain slapped his fingers lightly against the steering wheel. "Then it's time for a change!"

They reached the first home just as Carolyn was pulling in the driveway. "Courtney, how nice to see you!" she enthused as she got out. "Don't tell me these are your parents we're finding a home for?"

"They are indeed. Thanks for working with us. How's Coconut?" Carolyn, though she hadn't thought at first that she'd really want a pet at all, had ended up adopting a fluffy white cat named Coconut from the shelter. In fact, Courtney realized that would probably make Carolyn an excellent candidate for her video presentation, but she felt bad about asking considering how busy Carolyn already was.

"She's fabulous as always," the realtor replied with a smile. "She's the queen of the house, just as she deserves to be. And hello, Peppa. I'm sorry. I didn't mean to exclude you." She gave the big dog's head a pet.

"Oh, this is nice," Mrs. Cain said as they stepped into the house a few minutes later. "I like the wood."

Courtney followed along behind them as the group roamed through the house, but her mind was elsewhere. Looking at cabinets and porch railings and talking about the structure of the home only made her think of the dilapidated old bungalow that Julius Cline had purchased. It was odd enough to find the body of a wealthy man like Hugh McGowan in Curly Bay, but why *there* of all places?

"What do you think, Courtney?"

"Hmm?" She realized she hadn't been paying any attention at all.

"Do you think this would make a nice craft room?" her mother repeated. "Your father could put some shelving in the closet to hold all my supplies, and then there's this nice window that looks out over the backyard."

Randy Cain shook his head. "I'd have to put a new light fixture in here for you, too. There's not enough light, and your eyesight isn't what it used to be."

Mrs. Cain flicked her fingers playfully at her husband. "Like I need you to remind me! What do you think, Courtney?"

"I think it could be really great, Mom." The truth was, she hadn't had time to ask them what they wanted out of a new home. The craft room was a start, but there was probably more. She didn't want to let her parents down, and that meant she needed to pay more attention. That was difficult when the contest and Hugh McGowan's murder were already paying tug-of-war with her brain.

"I think we've seen it all," Carolyn announced as they looped back toward the entryway. "I'll just step outside and let you guys roam a little bit, see what you think of it."

Courtney followed her out the front door, realizing she had a potential opportunity to relieve herself of at least a little bit of the burden she was carrying around. "Could I talk to you for a second, Carolyn?"

"Of course," the realtor said with a smile. "If it's about that hideous stove that comes with the house, don't worry. It's old, but it works, and I know some landlords who'd be happy to buy it for their rental properties. They don't pay a whole lot, but it gets it out of your way."

"It's not that, although that's good to know." Courtney sucked in a deep breath of the spring air and glanced around at the landscaped flowerbeds and manicured front lawn. It really was a nice little house in a nice little neighborhood in a nice little town. It wasn't the sort of place where you'd think a murderer would hang out, nor a wealthy tycoon.

"Listen, I'm guessing you probably heard the news, and you already know that Hugh McGowan's body was found over on the east side of town."

The realtor crossed her arms in front of her chest and tipped her face back toward the sun. "You know, sometimes I wish I didn't watch the news. I hate to see things like that, even if it's people I don't know. But then I feel bad if I don't pay attention to what's going on. It's frustrating."

It was also frustrating to be the one who seemed to keep finding the bodies, but Courtney hadn't seen any mention of her name on the news report. She had a feeling she could thank Detective Fletcher for that one. "I was curious about something, and I thought you might be the best person to ask. You've got your finger on everything that goes on around here with the buying and selling of land, after all."

Carolyn tipped her head back forward and opened her eyes. She gave Courtney a sly smile. "You're wondering what someone like McGowan was doing in a place like this?"

"Well, yeah," Courtney admitted. She ran her thumb over the braided cotton of Peppa's leash. "The guy essentially made his living in real estate, even if it wasn't residential. I never thought of Curly Bay's real estate market as particularly booming."

"You're right about that," Carolyn laughed. "I do have a small tidbit of information for you, but I don't know that it will actually satisfy your curiosity. I did hear a rumor that Mr. McGowan was going to build somewhere in the area."

"Really?" Courtney practically screeched. "Here?"

"Yes, but–" Carolyn held up a cautionary finger "--like I said, it's a rumor. I never saw or heard anything official. I haven't seen any land purchases that would add up to that, so it makes me wonder if there was ever any truth to it at all. I don't like to assume things, especially not when we're talking about a man who's been killed."

"I understand," Courtney replied quickly. "Thank you."

As her parents came outside and began extolling the virtues of the covered porch, Courtney wondered where this clue fit in, and if it did at all. Was McGowan actually planning to build here? And if so, the question still remained as to why a man who'd worked in New York, London, and Paris, would even bother.

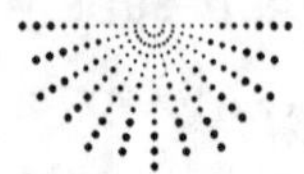

CHAPTER EIGHT

"Any luck with the presentation so far?" Jessi asked as they worked behind the building, letting the shelter dogs get out into the large playpens for some exercise. "Or maybe I should be asking if there's anything I can do."

Courtney shrugged as she watched a white lab mix named Clove streak toward one side of the fenced-in yard, put the brakes on just in time to miss the chain link, and then turn around and race off in the other direction. "I'm not sure there's much *I* can do."

"You always say that," Jessi pointed out. "When you've got something troubling you–whether it's something with the shelter, your personal life, or some wild mystery you've managed to get yourself embroiled in–you always think you won't be able to handle it. But you do. Every time. And you know we're always here to help."

"I know." Courtney smiled warmly at her coworker. She'd worked alongside people at Miller and Martinez Marketing who were perfectly nice when they spoke to you but who would easily stab you in the back just to get your desk when you weren't looking. Fortunately, her luck had been far better here. "When it comes to the contest, I'm just frustrated that I'm limited on time. I think we could make this a really great presentation if we just had an extra week or two."

"And the other stuff?" Jessi asked. She picked up a tennis ball and threw it for Billie, a border collie mix who was all about playing fetch.

"Mom and Dad have a few houses they liked, so they have some options to consider. I haven't heard much of anything from Detective Fletcher about the case, and I can't say that I have a lot of great leads myself. It's driving me crazy, but in the meantime, I'm trying to focus on what I can."

Jessi looked over her shoulder as a van pulled into the parking lot and stopped at the edge of the building where it wouldn't be in the way of any customers. She read the big sign on the side that said, "Cooper's Construction" and turned back to Courtney. "Does that involve having some repairs done? Because I have a whole list of things for you, boss."

Courtney managed a laugh as she called Clove over and clipped a leash onto her collar. The building constantly needed repairs, which really wasn't funny at all, but she'd been dealing with it long enough that it was more like a running joke than anything else. "Hopefully, we'll get around to them. Actually, I wanted Mark to give me a bid on adding a new wing."

"Wow, you really are serious about winning this money, aren't you?" Jessi gaped at her for a moment before she convinced Billie it was time to go inside. "That's big stuff!"

"Yes, but it's what this place has needed ever since I first started here. Getting this bid is actually part of my strategy. Can you put Clove up for me so I can go talk to him?"

"Sure thing!" Jessi grabbed Clove's lead in her free hand. "Come on, ladies! Let get inside and give someone else a chance at playtime!"

Mark Cooper had just stepped inside by the time Courtney made it to the lobby, and he held out his burly hand to shake hers. "Hey, Courtney. What seems to be the trouble this time?" Mark had done some other work for the shelter before, and he'd always seemed genuinely concerned about keeping the dogs and cats safe.

Courtney looked up at him, hoping beyond all hope that this wouldn't be a waste of time. "Well, there's a laundry list. But I actually wanted to see if you could give me a bid on a new wing."

The contractor's eyebrows shot up to the brim of his baseball cap. "Well, I'm not sure how to ask you this, but I'm going to anyway. How are you going to afford that? I don't mean any offense, but I know how this place struggles with money."

"It does indeed," Courtney admitted. Once more, she gave the rundown of the Change for Better competition. "My plan is to put together a video presentation with testimonials. I think it'll do well, but I also thought it might give us a leg up if we can explain *exactly* how we're using the money. Just saying we're going to do vague improvements doesn't mean much, but a specific bid that outlines everything might have more of an impact."

Mark nodded and unclipped his measuring tape from the side of his tool belt. "That sounds like a pretty good plan to me. Do you have any ideas as to what you'd like to do?"

"Oh, plenty of them!" Courtney pulled out a notebook she'd started quite some time ago, back when she'd first started at the Curly Bay Pet Hotel and Rescue and could already see just how much potential it had. She flipped past lists of ideas for making better use of the space they already had, notes about pricing on kennels and cages and carriers, and dozens of other ideas. Finally, she landed on several sketches she'd made that showed her vision of just what the shelter might look like if it was a little bigger.

Mark let out a low whistle. "You've been busy. Some of these look pretty good. Are they to scale?"

"As best as I could do it, although you're the expert." She bit her lower lip as she turned the notebook around and tapped on a page. "I don't know if you'd call this adding on a wing, necessarily, but I thought it might work. It's essentially bumping out the entire back side of the building. It would add a little bit to the grooming area, and then a whole lot to the shelter. That's where we really need the space."

"Maybe. May I?" Mark plucked a mechanical pencil from his pocket.

"Of course!" She watched as he easily sketched out some lines. They were slightly different than the ones that she'd come up with.

"This would take better advantage of the current shape and structure of the building, and you'd have less that would be torn up during the construction process," he explained.

"I like that," Courtney breathed as she studied the sketch. It was nothing more than a few lines on paper, but in her mind's eye she was already walking through wider hallways that led to bigger rooms. Most importantly, they would have a much greater capacity for the cats and dogs who so desperately needed homes. "I like it a lot, actually."

"Let's take a look around and do some measuring, then."

Courtney's excitement was only growing, but she could tell by the time they made it back to her office that Mark Cooper was feeling doubtful. He'd grown quieter as he made notes and measured doorways, and other than reaching in through a cage door to give a dog a pat on the head, he wasn't smiling at all.

"Give it to me straight," Courtney said, unwilling and unable to put up with the suspense any longer. "Is it impossible?"

He took the chair opposite her and slapped his notebook on his knee. "Not impossible, no. But it might not be likely to happen with the amount of money you're talking about potentially winning from this contest. Part of the problem is that the current structure needs repairs, so you have to consider more than just the addition."

"Oh." Courtney felt her shoulder sag a bit. "I was worried about that. I'm sorry if I wasted your time."

"Now, now, don't get too down on all this just yet. I need some time to run the final figures. You know I won't cut any corners that put anyone in danger, but we might be able to make something work. Give me a little time and I'll be sure to get back to you."

Courtney rose to walk him out. "Thank you. I really do appreciate it. If we do win this money, you'll be the first one I call."

He chuckled as he opened the side door of his van and deposited his tool belt inside. "And I'll make sure I move my schedule around to accommodate whatever we can. You're doing important work here."

"Thank you. Can I ask you something?"

Mark flipped his keys around in his hand and

wrapped his fingers around them to stop them from jangling. "Shoot."

Though she'd tried to shove it out of her mind as much as possible, Courtney's brain had continued to return to her other problems. It was inevitable, since they all had at least a little bit to do with construction. "Did you hear that rumor that Hugh McGowan was supposed to build something here? I thought you might've, being the only large contracting company."

He let out a hearty laugh that made his broad shoulders quiver. "That's a nice little fantasy, but it wouldn't ever come true. Not on my end, anyway."

She was intrigued, and now she wished she'd asked him about this earlier. "What do you mean?"

Mark adjusted the brim of his cap as he looked off in the distance down the road. "A rich guy like McGowan would bring in his own contractor and construction crew. He might hire one from the nearest city, but he sure wouldn't use a small-time guy like me."

"Even though you're right here?" Courtney was puzzled. That didn't seem like a good economic choice to her, but she hadn't built an empire of luxury resorts, either. "That's too bad."

"Yeah. A big investment like that would create all sorts of jobs and cash flow here locally, just in the construction, but it wouldn't happen. It's probably just as well that it didn't, although I don't mean to say the guy should've been killed. It just would've been some drama, that's all."

"I'm sure it would have," Courtney murmured.

"But, like I said, I'll work on this bid and see what I can come up with for you. I'll try to do it as quickly as possible so you can have it in time for your contest." He gave her a polite nod and hopped in his van.

She waved at him before she turned to go back inside. Every time she found out a little bit more about the mysterious Hugh McGowan and what he was doing here, it only brought up more questions. Courtney was desperate to know who killed him and why, but she hadn't quite been able to get to that part of the problem just yet.

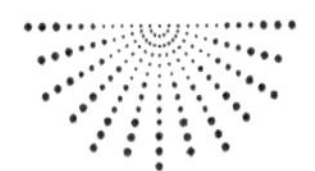

"What are you doing?"

Courtney glanced up from her spreadsheet at Dora and then went straight back to entering information. "I'm putting together the schedule for next week."

The groomer nodded. "Yes, and I see that you've already gone through all the bills, approved our paychecks, and ordered supplies."

"That's my job!" Courtney chirped.

Dora tapped a finger on the edge of the desk. "But you're doing it a little too quickly."

"There's a lot to do." Courtney flicked her eyes up at Dora again briefly, but she saw the inquiring look and decided her computer monitor was the safer bet.

"There always is," Dora agreed, "but you're working like a woman who's running out of time for something. I have a feeling you're trying to get things done so you can do something else without feeling guilty about it.

"You've got me," Courtney admitted.

Dora smiled. "You're not the only one who can put a few clues together. So, what's going on?"

Courtney pulled her hands off the keyboard and rested them in her lap. "Here's my thought. Mark Cooper was here yesterday, and he mentioned that *if* McGowan was going to build here, he wouldn't use local labor. He said it would probably make some people pretty upset. That made me wonder if someone might've been upset about the new community center being built."

"Why would anybody be mad about that? It should be a welcome addition, I'd think."

"I agree," Courtney replied, "except for *where* it's being built. That property Julius Cline purchased is in the middle of a residential neighborhood. Personally, I wouldn't want a busy place like that to be right in my backyard."

"Ah." Dora nodded her head as she put it together.

"So you're going to canvass the area and see what you can learn."

"Exactly, which is why I wanted to make sure I had some of this stuff done. I've been out of the office a lot, and I feel bad about that. I don't want to leave anyone in the lurch." She checked her monitor, filled in a few more cells, and saved the file.

"Don't worry about that. We've got it, and it's not as though we'll ever be 'caught up' working a job like this. I came to terms a long time ago with being perpetually behind, and I try to see it as a blessing. After all, it means I always have work to do." Dora winked. "Just let me know when you take off!"

An hour later, Courtney was pulling into the house next to the one Julius had purchased on Pine Street. This one was in much better condition, though it certainly wasn't new. She gathered up her file folder as well as the end of Peppa's leash as she got out of the car. The spring breeze pinged through the numerous windchimes hanging off the porch and rushed through the whirligigs in the yard. Peppa eyed them dubiously, but she followed along faithfully at Courtney's side.

"Yes?" The woman who answered the door was older. She had a stooped back, which made her look up at Courtney through the top of her glasses.

Courtney plastered a smile on her face, although her stomach was a bundle of nerves. "Hi, I'm Courtney. I'm the manager of the Curly Bay Pet Hotel and Rescue. I was wondering if I might be able to get your help with getting some grant money from a foundation called Change for Better." She launched into the spiel she'd been rehearsing so many times already, explaining how any testimonials from around town would help their cause.

The woman listened attentively, with her eyes dropping to Peppa now and then, and when Courtney finished, she opened the door wider. "Why don't you two just come on in and have some tea. I'd love to hear more about all this. I love dogs, but I don't have any of my own." She waved them into the house.

It was tiny and cramped inside, even with an open floor plan. Courtney could see why she didn't have pets here. One brush of Peppa's tail the wrong way and she'd brush something off the side table.

"My name is Dotty, by the way," the woman continued as she puttered around in the kitchen. "I don't get a lot of visitors, you know. My family moved away from here quite some time ago. That's actually why I'm looking forward to having that new community center next door. Maybe they'll have some senior citizen events. Give me something to do."

As Dotty returned with a tea tray, Courtney was happy to find an opening for exactly what she wanted to talk about. "I heard about that. Hopefully, they'll get it built quickly."

The older woman grazed her finger against her cheek with worry as she glanced toward the window. "Maybe. As soon as I heard it was happening, I started checking out my window every day, hoping to see some signs of construction. Real life is more exciting than television, you know. Anyway, the most exciting thing I've seen so far was just two men arguing, and then there were all the lights and sirens there a few days ago. I'm really looking forward to seeing them bringing out the heavy machinery, though."

Courtney's heart leaped up in her chest at this news. "Two men arguing? Do you know who it was?"

"No." Dotty shook her head in disappointment. "There's just enough distance from here, and with my old eyesight, I couldn't be sure. It probably wasn't anything as exciting as I'd want it to be, anyway."

That was too bad, but Courtney had a feeling Dotty might know more if she was as much of a busybody as she seemed to be. "It seems like a strange place for a community center, don't you think? Over here out of the way, amongst a bunch of houses." Courtney accepted a cookie from the tray Dotty handed her. She broke off a tiny crumb and gave it to Peppa.

"I do agree with that," Dotty replied with a firm nod. "I'm pleased about it, but I have a feeling Leon Bennett never would've sold the place to that man if he had any idea it was going to be a community center."

"So you know the former owner?" Courtney was bursting inside, but she tried to keep her hands from shaking as she put her teacup back on its saucer. This was it! Whoever had owned that old house must've discovered that Julius bought the place on false pretenses. He went over there to do something about it, but he mistook one man for the other and killed McGowan instead of Julius. That still didn't explain why the hotel tycoon was here at all, but Courtney could see all the pieces beginning to connect.

Dotty nodded. "Well enough. In fact, he lives just a few houses down. You see, the house next door used to belong to his father. Leon couldn't keep up with it anymore, but he hated to sell it. He thought that man he sold it to was going to fix it up nice."

Courtney checked her watch. "Dotty, thank you so much for your time and for the tea. I should really get going, since I have some other stops to make. If you know anyone who might be able to help us out with this contest, please pass along my information." After making sure Dotty had a flyer, her business card, and her profuse thanks, Courtney was headed off to find Leon Bennett.

Her heart thumped loudly in her chest as she approached the house Dotty had directed her to. There were no wind chimes or whirligigs here, just a plain little bungalow with peeling paint on the porch railing. She knew this was potentially dangerous. Maybe she should've contacted Detective Fletcher before she came her to confront the killer. She was already here now, though, and there was no turning back. She knocked on the door.

"Hang on!"

Courtney had a lot on her mind lately, but solving this mystery was the only thing that occupied it now.

She didn't know all the details yet, but she was about to confront a killer. He was taking forever to come to the door. Was he loading a gun? Hiding a knife in his belt? Escaping out the back door? She didn't have much of an escape plan herself, save for running away.

There was a heavy sliding noise as the deadbolt unlocked. The door slowly creaked open, revealing the back of a floral sofa in the living room and a muted television in front of it, tuned to an old black-and-white comedy. Courtney's heart was in her mouth as the door continued to open, revealing two dark eyes that stared at her.

"What can I do for you?" Leon Bennett asked genially. His arms shook as he gripped the sides of his walker, complete with tennis balls added to the bottom.

With his compression socks and orthopedic shoes, Courtney knew she wasn't looking at a killer at all.

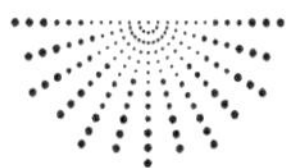

"So, what did you do?" Nathan paused with his fork and knife in the air.

"What could I do?" Courtney sighed. "I talked to him about the shelter, gave him a flyer, and apologized for making him get up. I did mention the community center, and he admitted he hadn't been too pleased about it at first, but he said his father probably would've been happy to know that his land was supporting the people of Curly Bay. In the end, I'm not really any closer to a solution."

"I'm sorry." Nathan cut off a tiny bit of steak and fed it to Archie, who was waiting patiently on the floor near his chair.

Courtney did the same for Peppa. "It's all right. I think I'm just letting myself get too stressed out about it. I really do appreciate dinner, by the way. It was amazing, as always." She put her utensils on her plate and took them into the kitchen. She and Nathan had spent enough time together over the last couple of years that she wasn't going to let him treat her like a guest even if he did cook dinner for her.

Nathan followed behind. They cleaned up, and then he poured a glass of wine for each of them. As they sat on the couch, Peppa and Archie curled up together on the floor nearby. "So, you want to run down your list of suspects with me?"

"It'd be a very short trip," Courtney admitted. "A lot of that is because I can't figure out why McGowan was in town in the first place. A man like him wouldn't have any business being in Curly Bay. Carolyn Davis said she heard a rumor he was going to develop something here, but that's a dead end considering she hasn't seen any land purchases that support it."

"You'd need a considerable amount of land for something like a hotel," Nathan agreed.

"I talked with Mark Cooper from Cooper Construction. He indicated that local construction workers would be upset about a build like that because McGowan likely wouldn't use them. He'd bring in workers from elsewhere. I can't imagine someone as kind as Mark Cooper offing McGowan himself, so that doesn't really get me anywhere, either."

Nathan swirled his wine in his glass. "I can definitely see the problem here. These things are all about connections, whether it's two people being in the same place at the same time, or whether they've known each other for years. You don't have any of that. I'd think someone would've spotted Hugh McGowan around town before he was killed, too."

"Maybe. I didn't really know anything about him. Mrs. Throgmorton only did because she travels so much. Plus she likes to keep up with the rich and famous. I'd just like to get through a day."

His dark blue eyes were full of concern as they traced her face. "You're really letting all of this stress you out, aren't you?"

Courtney pulled in a deep breath and sighed. "It's hard not to. Of course, I'm concerned about all this with McGowan. Then there's the whole thing about my parents buying a house."

"Have they made any decisions yet?" Nathan set his glass on a coaster.

"Not yet, which is just fine with me. There are only so many houses available in Curly Bay, and Carolyn showed them all the ones that might work for them. I don't think they've completely decided if they're going to move here or stay in the city. Anyway, I still want to help them as much as possible, but that's on hold for me until they decide what to do." Courtney finished off her glass of wine, feeling guilty.

"I hate to ask, but how's the presentation for the contest going?"

She sighed again. "It's not really going much of anywhere. I don't want to give up on it, but it's going to take too much time to put it all together. I haven't had the chance to talk to everyone I wanted to. I might just ask Connie if she can help me type up a nice letter and call it good enough, because at least that way I'd still have an entry. I'd feel like I was letting the shelter down if I didn't do that."

Nathan put his hand over hers and looked into her eyes. "If you want my opinion, and I'm going to give it to you anyway, you should just concentrate on what's most important to you."

Courtney raised a brow. "How am I supposed to do that? It's all important to me."

"I know it is, but it's okay if you aren't the one who

figures out what happened to Hugh McGowan. That's Detective Fletcher's job, and I'm sure he's working on it, too. He always seems to like your help, but it's okay if you're not the one to slap the virtual cuffs on the killer." He rubbed his thumb over her knuckles.

"Maybe."

"And it's also okay if you don't get this money for the shelter," he continued. "You give so much of your life to that place, which is commendable, but even the most amazing entry presentation is no guarantee that you'll win. Your parents will be okay if you aren't the one who guides them along in their home buying process."

"I can't just give up on it all," she replied, her brow furrowing.

"I don't mean that, and I know you better than to think you'd do such a thing. I'm just worried about you, and I want you to feel okay about taking a step back if you need to. You don't have to let it all rest on your shoulders."

Courtney rested her head on the back of the couch as she looked at him. She studied his sandy brown hair, the dark blue eyes that tipped down slightly at the outside corners, his rugged jaw that made him look more like a lumberjack or a firefighter than a web designer. He'd become one of her best friends, and she took great comfort in being near him. They didn't always have to talk, either. When they shared coffee in the mornings before work, sometimes they could simply sit in comfortable silence, knowing that each was there for the other. "I'll try, but I can't make any guarantees," she said with a smile.

He smiled back, letting out a little laugh. "I figured as much."

CHAPTER ELEVEN

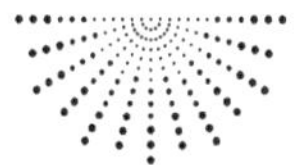

Courtney wove her car slowly through the suburban streets she'd grown up on. Not much had changed. The trees had grown, and a few houses had changed color with new siding. She'd come back home often enough that the little changes didn't really add up to much. The biggest difference she could see was how many people had already committed to moving out of the area. The purchases had been private offers, so it wasn't a matter of for-sale signs planted in the front yards. It was the presence of moving trucks, of open garages full of stacked cardboard boxes, of piles of unwanted items out on the curb with a sign that denoted them as free. It was very strange, but she reminded herself that nothing stayed the same. She certainly hadn't.

"Ah, there's my cupcake!" her father said when she and Peppa walked in the door. "I hope the traffic wasn't too bad."

"It was fine, Dad." She gave him a hug. "Do I smell fried chicken?"

"Just the stuff from the grocery store, I'm afraid," her mother said as she came out into the living room, drying her hands on a towel. "I feel bad that we invited you over to dinner and then didn't cook, but I've already packed up too much of my cookware!"

"I said you were going to need it," Randy reminded her.

"Oh, stop! Like you'd know how to get in here and make yourself a peanut butter sandwich." Cheryl flung the towel at her husband playfully. "Let's sit down."

Courtney looked around the familiar dining room, wondering how she'd really feel once this home no longer belonged to her parents. But, just as Jessi had told her, maybe it wasn't the home itself. After all, the wallpaper had been changed ten years ago. The ancient dining set they'd had when she was a kid, the one that bore her drawings on the underside of the table, had been switched for something much more modern. Even the stoneware was different. Though being here helped bring back some of those old times, things had already changed enough that it didn't really matter.

"So, what have you guys decided?" she asked as she reached for a chicken leg. Her mother had plated it all up on platters and in bowls instead of leaving it in the Styrofoam containers from the store.

Mr. Cain put a large serving of green beans on his plate. "We're definitely moving to Curly Bay," he announced proudly. "After spending a little bit of time there with you and Ms. Davis, we could see what a nice place it is. I think we'd be crazy not to go. Plus, we'd be a lot closer to you!"

"Don't worry, dear," her mother added. "We're not going to pop in at your place every evening. We know you have a life of your own, and we're going to respect that. But it certainly will make holidays easier."

Courtney shook her head and smiled. "Don't talk like that, Mom! I'm sure we'll see each other for more than just holidays. We can have a few lunches or dinners together each week. And who knows? I'll probably bump into you at the grocery store. Now, which house did you decide on?"

She thought about Nathan's advice, and how he'd

suggested that she handle what was most important. Courtney had felt a little bit frustrated at the idea, although she didn't doubt the wisdom of it. How could she possibly decide when everything felt vital? Right now, though, sitting at the table with her parents and helping them make a choice that would affect all of their futures, she knew this was a big one.

"That's the only part we're still debating. Oh, I forgot the biscuits. Hang on!" Her mother jumped up from the table and headed back into the kitchen.

"If you ask me, there's no debate at all," her father said. "That place on Kelly Street is the right choice no matter what. It has that nice little workshop out back where I can putter around and stay out of your mother's hair, and it has enough room for her crafts."

"So, what's the debate, then?" Courtney poked her fork at her mashed potatoes, imagining how nice it would be for her parents to come to a smaller community.

"The debate," her mother said as she came back in from the kitchen with the biscuits, "is that I'm worried it's too big. We want some space, yes. Otherwise, we'd move into one of those apartments for old people like us. But I'm worried about taking care of the yard and such."

Randy rolled his eyes. "I can still mow the lawn. And, with that yard being a little bigger, I can get one of those riding lawn mowers."

Her mother pursed her lips, but Courtney could tell it was only to hide her smile. "That's just what you'd like, wouldn't you?"

"You guys know I'm always around to help when I can," Courtney volunteered.

"We don't want you to have to do that!" her father insisted. "We're not moving to Curly Bay to be a burden on you. I figure if I get poorly and can't mow, I'll hire some teenage boy to do it. That's how I made money when I was growing up."

Cheryl nodded. "I suppose that's true."

A knock came on the door just as they were finishing up. It was Mrs. Rosenberg from next door. She was brimming over with excitement. "Sorry to come over unannounced, but I couldn't' wait to share the news. Oh, hi, Courtney! So nice to see you!"

"Nice to see you too, Mrs. Rosenberg." If Dotty was the busybody of her area of Curly Bay, then Mrs.

Rosenberg was the Gladys Kravitz of her parents' neighborhood. For as long as Courtney had known her, she'd spent most of her time finding out what everyone else was up to. In fact, Courtney was pretty sure Mrs. Rosenberg had decided to set up a neighborhood watch back in the day, simply so she had an excuse to see what other folks were doing.

"What's the good news?" her mother asked.

"I signed all the final closing papers!" Mrs. Rosenberg clapped her hands excitedly. "I have to say, I wasn't sure at first about all this. I mean, we've been in this neighborhood for a long time. But my house hasn't really felt the same since my husband passed away, and this is just the excuse I needed to finally move to Florida."

"Congratulations," Randy said sincerely. "Did everything go smoothly with the closing? We're about to do the same as soon as we make a final decision on our next home." He raised an eyebrow at his wife.

She made a face back at him and then smiled. "Sit down and tell us all about it, Virginia."

"Oh, well enough." Mrs. Rosenberg had a seat on the sofa at Mrs. Cain's suggestion. "It was actually supposed to happen a couple of days ago, but the man I've been speaking to said there was some sort of issue. Nothing with me or the house; it was all on their end. Something about one of their higher-ups being ill or something. But other than that, it was quick and easy! They came over to the house, pointed out all the places for me to sign, and I'll be heading to Florida in a couple of weeks!"

"That really was quick," Chery said. "Even with a little bit of a delay, this whole thing is happening fast.

"That's because we're talking about a massive corporation that's done this many times. They don't' come down and talk to us little people until they're really ready to get a move on. Of course, I've been documenting the whole thing ever since we first started seeing signs that something was happening."

Courtney scrunched her brows together, confused. "How did you know something was happening?"

"Oh, there are ways! I saw surveyors out here, measuring and marking, quite some time ago. Then all the suits came in. We didn't know what it was yet, and someone suggested they were widening the road, but I had a feeling it was something bigger. I've been documenting it this whole time. My nephew showed me how to put it all together in a photo album on my phone." Mrs. Rosenberg pulled it up and handed her mobile to Courtney.

She flicked through pictures showing men in yellow vests surveying the land, cars parked on the street that Mrs. Rosenberg probably didn't recognize, and finally the "suits" she'd referred to. They were standing out on the sidewalks or in the middle of the road, pointing, looking at paperwork, and talking seriously with each other. A shot of adrenaline bolted through her as she recognized their faces. She pointed at the one that was most definitely Julius Cline. "Do you know who these men are?"

Mrs. Rosenberg shook her head. "Not by name, no. Someone told me he was some sort of property investor. A good one, I guess, who specialized in turning cheap, undesirable land into something bigger and better."

"I see." Courtney flipped through the next few photos on the phone. That was definitely Julius Cline, and she had no doubt the man with him was none other than Hugh McGowan. She handed the device back.

Her parents and Mrs. Rosenberg continued to chat, but Courtney was running down a list in her mind. Julius Cline had purchased the land from Leon

Bennett under false pretenses. He'd told Connie Gilbert he was too busy for an interview due to a trip to New York, but he'd told Mrs. Throgmorton that he retired. Mrs. Throgmorton herself didn't know exactly what his job had entailed, other than the fact that it required a lot of travel. Then there was the phone call she'd overheard when she first met Julius, which was definitely about money. On that note, why would he need to enter the contest and get money for the community center if he was already wealthy? He had to have plenty of cash to throw around if he helped McGowan flip properties. Even more concerning was that he'd claimed Hugh was a stranger, but she'd just seen photographic evidence to the contrary.

"Excuse me a second," she said, rising and heading down the hallway. "I need to make a phone call." She slipped into her old bedroom and dialed a familiar number. "Detective Fletcher?"

CHAPTER TWELVE

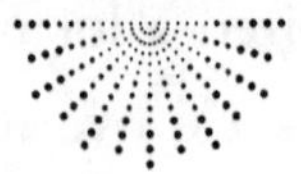

A few days later, Courtney sat at her desk at work. The notes she'd put together about the Change for Better contest were still there next to her keyboard, mocking her. The deadline had come and gone, rushing by, and there was nothing she could've done about it. Guilt wrung at her heart. What might she have been able to do for all these animals if she'd just spent more time? Or if she'd just tried to do things a different way?

With a heavy sigh, she picked them up and put them face-down in the recycle bin. Nathan was right. She couldn't let it all rest on her shoulders, and she'd done what she could. She'd done everything she could to help her parents find a new home, and they'd decided to go for the house on Kelly Street, even if it was a little bigger than they needed. And although the details hadn't come to light yet, Detective Fletcher had swiftly arrested Julius Cline for the murder of Hugh McGowan. That knocked out two of the three things that had been bothering her. As far as the shelter went, she couldn't be too upset. After all, she'd just gotten off the phone with a family that wanted to adopt a bonded pair of dogs for their kids to enjoy. She was still doing the work she'd set out to do, albeit a little slower and smaller than she'd like.

"Not working too hard, I hope." Nathan poked his head into the office.

Courtney looked up in surprise. "Of course I am! Oh, but I hope you're not here for lunch. I had Lisa on my calendar for today."

"I'm right here!" Lisa stepped in behind him, grinning from ear to ear.

"Me, too!" To Courtney's surprise, Connie Gilbert was waving at her from behind Lisa.

"And me!" Oliver Parker, the local photographer who took quality photos at cost for the shelter, stood next to Connie.

Courtney was confused, but everyone looked so happy that she couldn't stop a smile from spreading over her own face. "I must have seriously messed up my schedule. I guess we'll need a much bigger table at Russo's than I imagined."

"Only if you bring us, too!" Jessi and Dora stepped in from their respective sides of the building, and they were beaming as well.

Completely baffled at this point, Courtney swept her eyes around the room. "Someone here is going to have to tell me what's going on!"

"It's simple, really." Connie stepped forward, holding a flash drive in her hands. "You came to me and asked me to help you come up with some ideas for your presentation."

"But it's too late," Courtney replied, feeling guilty all over again. "The deadline has already passed."

"Well, we put something together anyway," Nathan explained. "You've done a lot for this town, and you'd be surprised how many people were interested in taking part." He handed the flash drive over to Jessi.

Jessi put it in the computer and opened the file. A video opened, and she expanded it so that it took up the entire screen. Connie's voice was narrating as shots of Main Street slid across the screen.

"Everyone thinks of small towns as being quiet, tight-knit communities where neighbors always help each other. That's true of Curly Bay, but there's one place that has done more for the community than most."

Courtney already felt herself tearing up when the screen switched to a shot of the front of the shelter. "Guys…"

"Just hold on!" Lisa pointed excitedly at the screen.

Realtor Carolyn Davis appeared on the screen, sitting in her pristine white living room with Coconut on her lap. She smiled prettily at the camera. "My name is Carolyn Davis, and I'm a realtor. It's my job to help people find their new homes, but Courtney and the others down at the Curly Bay Pet Hotel and Rescue help all the animals here in town find their new homes. I owe them so much, considering that my home simply wouldn't be the same without my sweet girl here." She stroked her fingers through the white cat's fur.

Next came Coach Malone from the high school football team. He was leaning against the chain link fence near the stands. "It would be hard to explain the difference I saw in my team when they started getting involved with these shelter animals. It took just one amazing dog to come in as a mascot, and all of a sudden, I saw their lives become much fuller as they started thinking about a world that's bigger than them, and even bigger than football."

Tears burned at the backs of Courtney's eyes. "You guys…"

But there was no time to say anything. Randy Shepard was now on the screen with his two dogs Mike and Ruthie at his sides. "These dogs completely changed my life. I didn't realize how much I needed them until they came along. They come with me to work every day, and all the kids who come to the park love seeing them. Ruthie here helped bring to life an old town legend, which is now getting its own museum right here in the park."

Courtney had to laugh a little bit as she remembered how Ruthie's constant howling had reminded everyone of the legend of the lake ghost. She thought the video was almost over, but the testimonials just kept coming. There was Reese Riley, the anchorwoman for the local TV station who often featured adoptable animals on her news program. Then there was Gladys, a homeless woman who now had her own source of income thanks to the dog clothes she made and sold at the shelter. Spencer Watson and Aimee Mitchell appeared with their little family, explaining how their desire to adopt the same dog had brought them together and shown them that they needed so much more than just a pet in their lives. Evelyn Howard, a local caterer, Ethan Perry, the new manager of the homeless shelter, Girl Scout leaders Leah Marsh and Linda Wheeler Nicholson, who'd come to volunteer at the shelter for a while, all had their stories to tell. Even Detective Fletcher had agreed to share a few stories.

Mrs. Throgmorton appeared on the screen, looking dignified as she held Sir Glitter in her lap. "I may not have adopted my dog from the shelter, but I can't begin to tell you how much of a purpose that Courtney and the shelter have given to my life. People think I'm perfectly happy because I have a little bit more money, but there's so much more in life that's important. Working with the Curly Bay Rescue has been the most meaningful thing I've ever done, and I live for it now."

Courtney could barely see through her tears.

Nathan rested a comforting hand on her shoulder. "Hang on. There's a really important one left you've got to see."

She sniffled as she returned her eyes to the monitor. It was Mark Cooper, standing in front of his van. He looked a little uncomfortable about being on camera. "All of us are putting this together without Courtney, the manager of the shelter, knowing about it. She very much wants to continue to help these animals, though, which in turn helps our entire community. In fact, she came to me asking how much it would cost to not only fix the current building but to add a new wing that would accommodate three times as many strays as they can right now. She hoped that having a definitive plan might help the Change for Better committee understand exactly where this money would be going. She's made one heck of a commitment, and I'm here to make one, too. If the Curly Bay Pet Hotel and Rescue wins this money, then I'll do all the repairs and additions at cost. I won't charge a penny more than it costs me, and my entire crew has already volunteered to put their time in without pay. We want this money to go as far as it possibly can. Thank you."

There was no chance of holding herself together any longer. The love and care that'd been put in that video was incredible and overwhelming. "I don't understand," she sobbed. "You guys did all this?"

Nathan put his arm around her. "We all knew how important it was to you, but that you simply didn't have the time. Nobody who puts as much time and effort as you do into this place could possibly pile more onto her plate, and yet you do."

"Writing up a letter just wouldn't be enough," Connie explained. "It would be nice, but we got together, and we knew that your original idea would be the best. That's when we brought Oliver in."

The photographer smiled bashfully. "I don't usually have much chance to work on my videography skills, but I think I did all right."

"It was wonderful," Courtney gushed. "You've always done so much for us!"

"You already did a lot when it came to contacting people," Jessi said. "Dora and I easily did the rest simply by looking through the files. As soon as we told them it was for you, they were happy to agree. Oliver and Connie did a lot of the footwork when it came to going around and getting it all actually done."

Courtney looked around at all these people that she loved so much. They were people who cared about this shelter just like she did, and they obviously cared about her, too. "This was so sweet. I don't know what to say."

"So, you really did like it?" Lisa asked with a smile.

"Of course I did!" Courtney pressed a tissue to her cheek.

"Good," her best friend replied, "because we submitted it five minutes before the deadline!"

"You're kidding!" But she knew they weren't, and Courtney wanted to scream from the rooftops in pure joy. She hugged everyone several times over, never having felt so loved and supported in her entire life. They might not win the money, but simply knowing that she had the community at her back like that was everything she ever could've asked for.

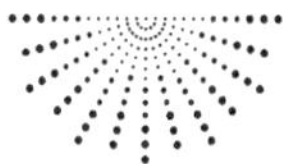

CHAPTER THIRTEEN

"Right over there. Just like that. Good." Mark Cooper gave the okay sign to one of his workers as he unloaded a large truckload of trusses. He turned to Courtney and grinned. "What do you think?"

"I think I've been smiling for so long that my cheeks are going to fall off," she admitted. The weather was getting cooler, but it made for perfect construction weather as Mark and his workers started on the new wing of the shelter. "It's going to be amazing."

"I think so," he agreed. "And we won't have a problem at all making sure it happens with the budget we've got to work with. I always get a contractor's rate at the lumber yard, but they decided to give me an even better discount when they found out what this was all for. I don't think there's a single person in Curly Bay who doesn't know about this project."

Courtney shook her head, once again blown away by all the kindness everyone had shown. She'd been constantly struggling to raise funds and find volunteers ever since she'd started this job, but it was like the road had leveled out and everything was going to be a smooth ride from now on. "That's wonderful. And thank you so much. I don't think we ever would've gotten this grant if it weren't for you."

Mark's cheeks turned a little pink. "Don't say that! I did what I could, but this was really all about you. You were the one who brought this place to life and really made it mean something to folks." Someone shouted at him from the other side of the construction zone. "Excuse me."

"Of course." Courtney had plenty to do, anyway. As excited as she was about the new wing, that didn't mean there wasn't still lots of old business. There were always supplies to be ordered and bills to be paid. She stepped into her office and found Detective Fletcher waiting for her. He had a little chihuahua mix in his lap as he sat in the chair across from her desk.

"I see Pickle found you," she noted as she crossed the room. "Is Artemis ready for a new friend?"

Detective Fletcher smiled at the little dog, but he shook his head. "No, Jessi put him in my arms on her way through. She said she had something to do, and she'd be right back, but I haven't seen her for a few minutes. He looks comfortable, though."

She sat down. "Is there something I can do for you? Or are you just here for the snuggles?"

He stroked one large finger down the little dog's head. Pickle looked like he was about to fall asleep. "I actually just came in to give you an update. It took a while to get everything out of Julius Cline. He's pretty wealthy, and he hired some good lawyers."

"Oh." Courtney sat up a little straighter. She'd been so distracted by the construction and a few other things going on in her life that she hadn't had much time to give it any thought. "I'm listening."

Detective Fletcher sighed. "As I'm sure you've figured out, Julius had been Hugh McGowan's partner for a long time. He was more of a silent partner. He was good at what he did, finding properties that had good potential, but he didn't want the fame that went along with it."

"I guess that explains why nobody really knew what he did for a living," Courtney murmured.

He nodded. "Cline decided it was time to retire. As rich as McGowan was, he didn't like the idea of giving up his cash cow just yet. He'd made so much money on Julius that he didn't want to let him go and bring his empire to an end. He convinced Julius that he owed him one more job."

Courtney leaned forward. "So, they actually were going to build a hotel?"

"Yes, but it's probably not what you think. Cline purchased Leon Bennett's land under the ruse of a community center, because he knew nobody would ever sell it to him if they knew the real reason. *That* was where they were going to build a hotel, and they'd probably have ended up buying out the land around it as well."

"Just like McGowan was doing in the city, where my parents used to live," Courtney breathed.

"Indeed, except they were being a little more underhanded about it until McGowan's legal team could seal the deal so tightly that nobody could say a word about it. It turns out Julius was already frustrated with this, because he didn't like cheating the citizens of his own town. McGowan continued to pressure him, though, wanting more and more. Julius realized this wasn't going to be the last job, after all, not if Hugh had anything to do with it, and so he killed him."

"Wow." Courtney slumped a little in her seat, wondering if it'd really been worth it to either one of them. "What's going to happen to the land now?"

This brought a small smile to Detective Fletcher's face. "Fortunately, just before he went off to prison, Cline donated the land he'd purchased to the city. A community center will be built there after all."

"That's wonderful. Thank you so much for telling me." Courtney truly felt relieved that everything had come to the light of day.

"Not a problem. Now, then." Fletcher carefully scooped the little dog out of his lap and handed him over to Courtney with a wink. "I've got to get back to the station and take care of some things. You stay out of trouble."

"I'll do my best."

That evening, Nathan walked over from his house. He had Archie on a harness, which the fluffy orange cat didn't quite seem to appreciate judging by the look on his face, though he was willing enough to tolerate it if it meant he got to go a few places. "You ready?"

Courtney felt butterflies zipping through her stomach as she took one last glance in the mirror by the door. "I think so. I'm a little nervous, though."

"There's nothing to be nervous about," he said in his usual calm, comforting voice.

Courtney looked at him, knowing he was absolutely right. They were having dinner with her parents as a nice little housewarming party to help them get settled in their new home in Curly Bay. It was a great place that would suit them perfectly, and they were already getting unpacked far faster than Courtney had ever imagined. "You're right."

Nathan raised an eyebrow at her. "How do you think they'll take the news?"

It was impossible for her to suppress a smile as she once again studied the diamond ring on her finger. She'd looked at a thousand times ever since Nathan had asked her to help get Archie's collar off and she'd found it looped into the buckle. She'd known for a long time that Nathan was the right person for her, and she was pretty sure her parents might've known even before she did. "I have a good feeling they're going to be thrilled. I know I am." She pressed her lips to his.

When they rounded up Peppa and Archie and the four of them piled into the car, Courtney felt a deep sense of satisfaction settle over her shoulders and down into her chest. At one point, she'd thought her life had been turned completely upside down. Now, she knew it was only getting shaken up so that she could find the path she was supposed to be on. It was time for yet another celebration and yet another chapter in Courtney's life. She'd helped lots of animals find the place where they belonged, and here in Curly Bay with Nathan was her true forever home.

THANK YOU FOR CHOOSING A PUREREAD BOOK!

We hope you enjoyed the story, and as a way to thank you for choosing PureRead we'd like to send you this free Special Edition Cozy, and other fun reader rewards…

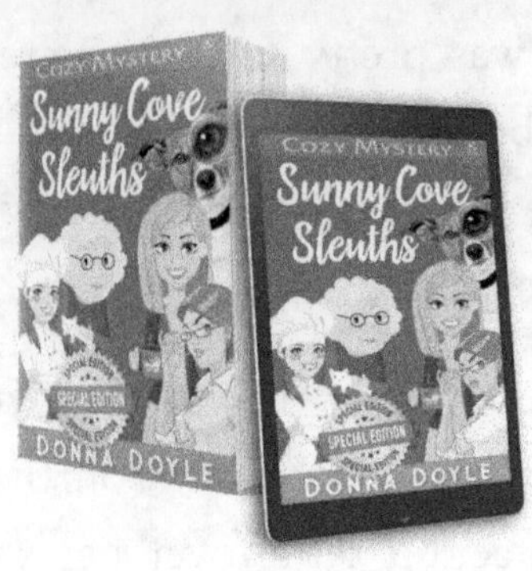

Click Here to download your free Cozy Mystery
PureRead.com/cozy

Thanks again for reading.

See you soon!

The Missing Pom Mystery

The Case of the Confused Canine

A Case Full of Cats

A Furry case of Foul Play

The Case of a Beagle and a Body

A Case of Canines, Cats, & Costumes

A Case of Frauds and Friendly Lizards

A Very Furry Christmas Mystery

The Mysterious Case of Books, Barks, & Burglary

A Shocking Case of Party Animals

A Strange Case of Pretty Puppies and Petty Theft

The Troubling Case of Summer Punches & Picnic
Puppies

A Feisty Case Of Festive Murder

A Catty Case of Mayor's Murder

The Suspicious Case Of A Dog Spa Crime

The Mystery of the Hapless Hound of Curly Bay

The Strange Case of the Shelter Dog Suspect

The Cozy Case of Murder and A True Furever Home

Also, be sure to join our Reader Club (100% free)

PureRead.com/cozy

COZY MYSTERY
Sunny Cove
Sleuths
SPECIAL EDITION
DONNA DOYLE
COZY MYSTERY
Sunny Cove
Sleuths
SPECIAL EDITION
DONNA DOYLE

At PureRead we publish books you can trust. Great tales without smut or swearing, but with all of the mystery and romance you expect from a great story.

Be the first to know when we release new books, take part in our fun competitions, and get surprise free books in your inbox by signing up to our Reader list.

As a thank you you'll receive this exclusive Special Edition Cozy available only to our subscribers...

Click Here to download your free Cozy Mystery
PureRead.com/cozy

Thanks again for reading.
See you soon!